D1342040

Tutankhamun
and the
Golden Chariot

First published in 2007 by
Franklin Watts
338 Euston Road
London
NW1 3BH

Franklin Watts Australia
Level 17/207 Kent Street
Sydney
NSW 2000

A CIP catalogue record for this book is available
from the British Library.

ISBN 978 0 7496 7084 9 (hbk)
ISBN 978 0 7496 7415 1 (pbk)

Series Editor: Melanie Palmer
Series Advisor: Dr Barrie Wade
Series Designer: Peter Scoulding

Printed in China

Franklin Watts is a division of
Hachette Children's Books.

HOPSCOTCH HISTORIES

Tutankhamun
and the
Golden Chariot

By Damian Harvey and Graham Philpot

W
FRANKLIN WATTS
LONDON•SYDNEY

About this book

Some of the characters in this book are made up,
but the subject is based on real events in history.
A young boy named Tutankhamun became King of Egypt
in 1333 BCE. He was probably about 8 years old when
he became King and ruled for almost 10 years. We know
little about his short life, but he spent most of his time in
a palace near modern-day Cairo, until he unexpectedly
died at the age of 18. We found out more about him in
1922 CE, when his tomb was found by a British explorer
named Howard Carter. In the tomb there were many
treasures including a throne and a golden chariot.

When Tutankhamun was eight
years old, his father, the Pharaoh,
gave him a golden chariot.

"It is the best chariot in the whole of Egypt, Tut," said the Royal Vizier.

"It is a chariot fit for a king,"
said the Pharaoh.

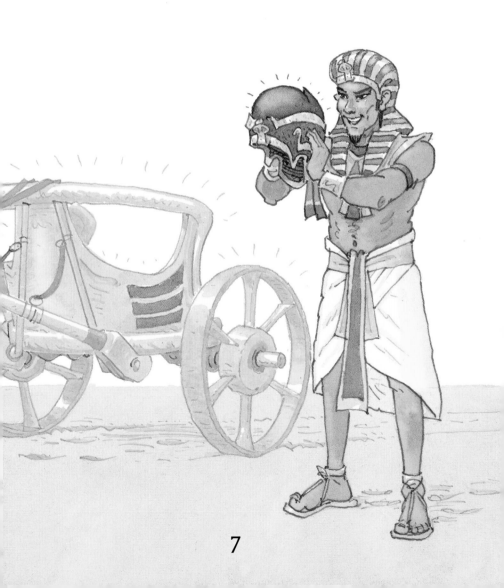

"Can I try it now?" asked Prince Tut.
"No!" said the Vizier. "Not until
after your lessons."

"The Vizier is right," said the
Pharaoh. "You have a lot to
learn, because one day you
will be Pharaoh, King of Egypt."

Prince Tut studied hard every day. He enjoyed his lessons but looked forward to the end of the day. Then he could ride his chariot.

Every night, he would race his golden chariot around the palace gardens as fast as he could.

One day, Prince Tut heard a noise
outside the palace. He ran to the
window and saw a crowd had
gathered along the road.

12

Tut had to stand on tiptoe to see what was happening.

Three soldiers were riding their chariots fast along the road, racing each other.

It was the most exciting thing
Tut had ever seen!

15

Prince Tut wanted to race his
chariot against the best of the
soldiers. But he was not allowed
to ride outside the palace gardens.

16

"It is too dangerous for a young
prince," said the Vizier.

17

Prince Tut waited until it was getting dark. Then he crept from his room and down to the stables to find his chariot.

When he reached the stables, Tut
found his chariot ready. He led the
horse out as quietly as he could,
hoping no one would hear.

21

When he got to the gardens, Tut was amazed to find that the palace gates were wide open.

As quickly as he could, he rode out
of the palace and through the city
without being seen.

Prince Tut arrived just in time
for the soldiers' secret race.
"Wait for me!" he cried.

The soldiers did not recognise
Tut. "You're just a boy," they
laughed. "You'll never beat us."

But after riding his chariot around the palace gardens, Tut found it easy racing along a big road. He soon left the soldiers far behind.

27

Tut crossed the finishing line first!
Then he disappeared into the
night, and no one ever knew
who the young driver was.

People talked for years afterwards
about the wonderful golden
chariot that had appeared
one night.

Many years later, an explorer called Howard Carter discovered Tut's tomb hidden in the Valley of the Kings.

The tomb was filled with lots of wonderful treasures, including Tut's golden chariot.

Hopscotch has been specially designed to fit the requirements of the National Literacy Strategy. It offers real books by top authors and illustrators for children developing their reading skills. There are 49 Hopscotch stories to choose from:

Marvin, the Blue Pig
ISBN 978 0 7496 4619 6

Plip and Plop
ISBN 978 0 7496 4620 2

The Queen's Dragon
ISBN 978 0 7496 4618 9

Flora McQuack
ISBN 978 0 7496 4621 9

Willie the Whale
ISBN 978 0 7496 4623 3

Naughty Nancy
ISBN 978 0 7496 4622 6

Run!
ISBN 978 0 7496 4705 6

The Playground Snake
ISBN 978 0 7496 4706 3

"Sausages!"
ISBN 978 0 7496 4707 0

The Truth about Hansel and Gretel
ISBN 978 0 7496 4708 7

Pippin's Big Jump
ISBN 978 0 7496 4710 0

Whose Birthday Is It?
ISBN 978 0 7496 4709 4

The Princess and the Frog
ISBN 978 0 7496 5129 9

Flynn Flies High
ISBN 978 0 7496 5130 5

Clever Cat
ISBN 978 0 7496 5131 2

Moo!
ISBN 978 0 7496 5332 3

Izzie's Idea
ISBN 978 0 7496 5334 7

Roly-poly Rice Ball
ISBN 978 0 7496 5333 0

I Can't Stand It!
ISBN 978 0 7496 5765 9

Cockerel's Big Egg
ISBN 978 0 7496 5767 3

How to Teach a Dragon Manners
ISBN 978 0 7496 5873 1

The Truth about those Billy Goats
ISBN 978 0 7496 5766 6

Marlowe's Mum and the Tree House
ISBN 978 0 7496 5874 8

Bear in Town
ISBN 978 0 7496 5875 5

The Best Den Ever
ISBN 978 0 7496 5876 2

ADVENTURE STORIES

Aladdin and the Lamp
ISBN 978 0 7496 6692 7

Blackbeard the Pirate
ISBN 978 0 7496 6690 3

George and the Dragon
ISBN 978 0 7496 6691 0

Jack the Giant-Killer
ISBN 978 0 7496 6693 4

TALES OF KING ARTHUR

1. The Sword in the Stone
ISBN 978 0 7496 6694 1

2. Arthur the King
ISBN 978 0 7496 6695 8

3. The Round Table
ISBN 978 0 7496 6697 2

4. Sir Lancelot and the Ice Castle
ISBN 978 0 7496 6698 9

TALES OF ROBIN HOOD

Robin and the Knight
ISBN 978 0 7496 6699 6

Robin and the Monk
ISBN 978 0 7496 6700 9

Robin and the Friar
ISBN 978 0 7496 6702 3

Robin and the Silver Arrow
ISBN 978 0 7496 6703 0

FAIRY TALES

The Emperor's New Clothes
ISBN 978 0 7496 7077 1 *
ISBN 978 0 7496 7421 2

Cinderella
ISBN 978 0 7496 7073 3 *
ISBN 978 0 7496 7417 5

Snow White
ISBN 978 0 7496 7074 0 *
ISBN 978 0 7496 7418 2

Jack and the Beanstalk
ISBN 978 0 7496 7078 8 *
ISBN 978 0 7496 7422 9

The Three Billy Goats Gruff
ISBN 978 0 7496 7076 4 *
ISBN 978 0 7496 7420 5

The Pied Piper of Hamelin
ISBN 978 0 7496 7075 7 *
ISBN 978 0 7496 7419 9

HISTORIES

Toby and the Great Fire of London
ISBN 978 0 7496 7079 5 *
ISBN 978 0 7496 7410 6

Pocahontas the Peacemaker
ISBN 978 0 7496 7080 1 *
ISBN 978 0 7496 7411 3

Grandma's Seaside Bloomers
ISBN 978 0 7496 7081 8 *
ISBN 978 0 7496 7412 0

Hoorah for Mary Seacole
ISBN 978 0 7496 7082 5 *
ISBN 978 0 7496 7413 7

Remember the 5th of November
ISBN 978 0 7496 7083 2 *
ISBN 978 0 7496 7414 4

Tutankhamun and the Golden Chariot
ISBN 978 0 7496 7084 9 *
ISBN 978 0 7496 7415 1

* hardback